# I Am a Home Schooler

## Julie Voetberg

*Hand-tinted photographs by* Taasha Owen

ALBERT WHITMAN & COMPANY
MORTON GROVE, ILLINOIS

*With a thankful heart to my mom, my family, and God. J.V.*
*For my family, my friends..., and Tom. T.O.*

Library of Congress Cataloging-in-Publication Data
Voetberg, Julie.
I am a home schooler / written by Julie Voetberg ; illustrated by
Taasha Owen.
p. cm.
Summary: Describes the experiences of a nine-year-old girl who is
taught by her mother on their farm in Washington State.
ISBN 0-8075-3441-2 (lib. bdg.)
ISBN 0-8075-3442-0 (pbk.)
1. Home schooling—Juvenile literature. 2. School children—Juvenile
literature. [1. Home schooling. 2. Family life—Washington (State)]
I. Owen, Taasha, ill. II. Title.
LC40.V64 1995

649'.68—dc20                                                95-2562
                                                              CIP
                                                               AC

The text of this book is set in Sabon.
Hand-tinted photographs are by Taasha Owen.
Design is by Karen A. Yops.

My name is Teigen. I'm nine years old, and I am a home schooler. That means I do my schoolwork right here at home. My mom does most of the teaching, and my three little sisters are my classmates. I've never even been to a regular school.

Even though I stay home, I get up at seven, just like kids who go to regular schools. First Mom, my sisters, and I all sit on the couch together and start our day with prayer. Then I help Mom make breakfast and get my sisters ready for the day. Dad leaves for work before the sun rises, so Mom needs my help.

After breakfast I begin my chores. We live in the country on a little farm that has a barn, a creek, a pond, and lots of animals. Mom and Dad say that caring for my pets is part of my education. It teaches me to be responsible.

Each morning I go to the barn. I give Misty some fresh hay, check her water, and brush her coat. Misty is my pony. I bought her last summer with money I saved. It's also my job to keep her stall clean. Next I give the bunnies food and water and sometimes a special treat like apples or carrots. Then I say hello to some of the other animals. I toss extra hay to the goats and say good morning to Albert, the barn cat.

My sister Michal, who is six, has chores, too. She feeds the chickens and collects the big brown eggs each day. Sometimes she lets me help. My littlest sisters, Soryn and Prentice, are only four and two. They don't have any chores, but they like to tag along.

Then it's time to practice the piano. I don't always want to, but I know that if I do, I might be able to play pretty well someday. I like it when my teacher, Mr. Cummings, is proud of me. He helps me to learn new songs and teaches me about famous composers. He comes to my house once a week, but I have to practice every day.

Next I do math. That's my hardest subject. I do my problems from a textbook, just like my friends in regular school. I like fractions and story problems, but I don't like memorizing my multiplication tables! Some days we go to the kitchen for my lesson. We bake, and that helps me with my fractions, because I have to do a lot of measuring and adding. Mom is good at making math more fun.

After math I work on my reading and English lessons. Reading and writing are my best subjects. I've read a lot of books this year. My favorites are *The Little Princess, The Boxcar Children, Gone with the Wind,* and *The Black Stallion.*

Most of the time I use a workbook for English. This week I'm doing the part on writing a report. I'm learning how to find information and put it together so that it makes sense. Sometimes I write letters or thank-you notes for my lessons, or stories and poems with pictures to go along with them.

When I'm finished, I take a short break. That's when I get a snack or a drink of water and sharpen my pencils.

Next I practice my penmanship and memorize my spelling list. I'm learning cursive now. I copy my lesson in my best writing, and Mom checks it. If it isn't good enough, I have to do it over again! Spelling is easy for me, so I work from a fifth-grade speller. I don't take tests in my other subjects, since Mom knows how I'm doing, but I take a spelling test each Friday. I get most of the words right.

Mom says one of the good things about home schooling is that I can go at my own pace. That means I can skip the lessons I already know well or slow down when I need extra time. I like home schooling because nobody laughs when I make a mistake, and Mom always has time to answer my questions.

Maybe you're wondering what my sisters are doing while Mom is teaching me. Well, they have "schoolwork," too. We have a special cupboard full of games, puzzles, markers, stamps, flashcards—all kinds of good things! They can choose something to play with while I'm working with Mom. Sometimes they bother me when I'm studying but that's just part of being a family. We have to learn to work together.

Now that Michal is six, she has her own phonics and math workbooks. Mom spends time with her each day, and I teach her, too. I can help her read words she doesn't know and listen to her practice counting by fives.

Sometimes all of us learn together. When we studied how the Pilgrims settled in America, we checked out library books and tapes about them. We made Pilgrim costumes and cooked some of the foods Pilgrims ate, like pumpkin pie and cornbread. My sisters had as much fun as I did, and we all learned a lot.

By now it's getting close to lunch. I often have enough time to play a geography game or see one of our science videos. Today I watched one about how animals survive in the desert. Did you know that a male sand grouse has feathers that soak up water? He can fly back to his chicks, who peck at him to take a drink. Neat!

I usually finish all my work by lunchtime. Maybe that's because I don't spend time changing classrooms, going to recess, or waiting for the teacher to help me.

After lunch is cleaned up, my sisters and I have a quiet time. We're all ready for a rest, and Mom is, too! I choose a few books and settle down to read. I love poetry, mysteries, and true stories about famous people in history. Today I'm reading about the life of Laura Ingalls Wilder.

We rest for an hour and a half, so if I get tired of reading, I pull out my art set and draw. I'm writing a play, and I like drawing pictures of the characters in it.

It's great to have free time in the afternoon! If the weather is nice, I go outside. Since most of my home schooler friends are done with school by lunchtime, they can come over to play. We build hay forts in the barn and push each other on the tire swing. We can ride Misty or play dress-up. If it's cold and wet, we

stay inside and make paper dolls or paint and color.

Mom does most of her housework in the afternoon, and I help out. I fold laundry and put it away and unload the dishwasher. I straighten the bookshelves or read stories to my sisters while Mom's getting dinner.

After dinner, Dad looks over my work. We talk about what I learned and if I had a good day. He wants to know if I helped my little sisters and if I was a good example to them. I don't have homework, but sometimes we practice my times tables together, or I recite what I'm memorizing. Right now I'm learning "The Highwayman," a poem by Alfred Noyes.

If Dad has time, he plays checkers with me or shows me how to use his tools. He taught me to make a geo-board all by myself!

Mrs. Miltmore, the art teacher, visits twice a month. Three other home schoolers come over, and she gives us art lessons. She brings lots of supplies and tells us how to use them. I asked her to teach me to draw a horse, and my picture turned out great. I love art almost as much as I love to read!

On Thursdays my sisters and I go to a class just for home schoolers. We call it "Co-op," which is short for "cooperation." That's because all the moms and kids cooperate to have a great day together. There are over one hundred students, and I've made a lot of new friends. We rent a big church building that has a gym and classrooms. We divide up into groups according

to our ages. The youngest kids stay in the same class the whole time, but the older groups take turns going to gym, science, and history.

In gym we do exercises and play games; in science we're making solutions that will form crystals; and in history we're learning what life was like for the American colonists.

Home schoolers get together with kids in regular school, too. We can play in our public schools' bands or be on their sports teams, and some of us take after-school skating or gymnastics lessons.

Sometimes we go on field trips with other home schoolers. Once we went to visit a mint factory that's in our town. I learned that the factory makes different flavorings like peppermint and spearmint from plants and sends them all over the world. Other factories use the flavorings to make gum and candy. When we visited the fire department, Firefighter Allen showed us the aid car and some of the life-saving equipment he uses. My friend Kyle tried on the neck brace. It keeps an injured neck still and protects it until the aid car gets to the hospital.

So you can see home schoolers meet lots of people and don't just sit at home!

Days don't always go just as we planned. One morning Michal fell off her bunk bed and cut her chin. She had to go to the emergency room and get seventeen stitches! We didn't do *any* schoolwork that day.

Another time, our dog threw up on the rug, and Mom needed to clean it up. Meanwhile, Prentice couldn't get her overalls off and went to the bathroom on the floor. She was crying *loud*. When Soryn ran to help, she fell and smacked her head on the sink. It seemed like everyone was crying! Mom said I could put my work away for a while and that we could all go for a nature walk instead. Yay!

Sometimes we change our plans when we find something interesting to learn about. On a walk one afternoon, we discovered some dried owl pellets on the trail. Owl pellets are small blobs of bone and fur that the owl burps up after eating an animal. When we poked the pellets apart with sticks, we could see the tiny bones of the animal the owl had for dinner. We spent a lot of time with those owl pellets. I'm glad there was no school bell out on the trail to interrupt that lesson. We wanted to find out more about owls, so Mom took us to the library for books and a science video.

Another day, in spring, we hiked down to the pond to collect frog eggs. Later, we watched the eggs hatch and the tadpoles grow legs. Then we let the tadpoles go. I read in my encyclopedia that the change from an egg to a frog is called metamorphosis. This year, for our home school science fair, I'll make a chart that shows all I've learned about the life cycle of a frog.

Every now and then, Dad takes Michal and me to his sawmill. We watch as he picks up a big log with the forklift and puts it on the mill. The blade moves down the log and comes back, pushing the newly cut board with it. Dad stacks the board on the lumber pile, and then he's ready to cut another one. I think I'm lucky to be able to spend time with my dad at his job. It's good to be with him, and I like watching the huge log turn into a neat stack of lumber.

In May it's time for me to plant my garden. I like growing cucumbers and sweet peas best. We've done experiments, so I know just what my seeds need to grow into strong and healthy plants. Once we put bean plants in a big box with a small hole cut in the top. No matter where they were in the box, the plants always grew toward the hole. That taught me how much plants need light.

Our school year ends in July, when our garden is getting ready to harvest. The whole family works together to keep it weeded. Then we pick and clean the fruits and vegetables and help Mom can or freeze them.

While other kids are back at school in the fall, I'm packing for our vacation. This September we traveled all the way to Wyoming to visit Yellowstone National Park. We saw moose and bison and miles and miles of burned forest land. A terrible forest fire destroyed much of the park a few years ago. We went to Old Faithful and learned that she shoots a stream of water one hundred feet into the air every sixty-five minutes—faithfully! At the lodge nearby, Dad bought me a jackknife as a souvenir. He's trying to teach me to whittle, but I haven't quite got the hang of it yet.

When we come home from vacation, we get organized for the new school year. By early October, we're ready to start.

In our state, Washington, home schoolers take a test at the end of the year, just like kids in regular school. Some kids take it at home, and some, like me, take it with other home schoolers. The test results tell me and my family what I've learned and where I might need extra practice.

I work hard to get good scores. Tests like these show that all over the country, home schoolers are doing really well.

Sometimes I wish I could go to regular school or ride on a school bus. I think recess on a playground sounds like fun. But learning at home is exciting. My whole day seems full of interesting things to discover. I wouldn't want to miss Co-op, and it's good to be with my family—they need me! So for now, I'm happy to be a home schooler.

# ABOUT HOME SCHOOLING

Parents who home school are frequently asked to explain why they have chosen it over a more traditional education. The reasons vary from family to family, but a common theme is the desire by parents to take more responsibility for how and what their children are learning, and to be able to spend more time with them. Many parents want the freedom to include a curriculum that accords with their own spiritual values, while others are concerned about the quality of education, or about violence, drugs, and gangs in today's schools.

For various reasons, some children experience academic or social failure in traditional schools. Such children may thrive in the home school setting. In addition, some families have special circumstances that home schooling can best accommodate, such as residence in remote areas or parents who work "on the road."

There are about one million home schoolers in the United States. The number has increased by 25 percent every year since 1990. There is no "average" home schooling family. Some parents will home school all of their children from kindergarten through twelfth grade, while others may choose home schooling for only one of their children and then only for a limited time during the elementary or secondary years.

Each state has different guidelines for parent qualification. For example, two states permit any parent who wishes to home school to do so; several require parents teaching at the high-school level to be certified teachers or be overseen by a certified teacher. (Requiring all parents to have teacher certification would render many otherwise-qualified parents ineligible to educate their children.)

To help parents, some states offer workshops on locating teaching resources, recognizing learning styles, and understanding the legal aspects of home schooling. And many parents call on outside resources, such as tutors, to teach subjects in which they do not feel qualified.

Home schooling is legal in every state, and more than one-half of the states require standardized testing for evaluation purposes. In these tests, home schoolers consistently score 15 to 30 percent higher than the national average.

This success, combined with the understanding that families have been effectively home schooling for hundreds of years (Thomas Edison, Pearl S. Buck, and several U.S. presidents, including Abraham Lincoln, were home schooled), has brought growing acceptance of home schooling as a valid alternative to traditional education.